CURIOUS CALVIN
by TONY GARTH

Calvin had always been curious.

He wanted to know absolutely everything...

He often wondered why bees were stripy?

And why the apples in his garden were red, but the ones next door were green?

It was all very puzzling.

It didn't stop there.

Why were all the socks in his Dad's sock drawer black?
What was the point in that?

And where was the zebra from the zebra crossing outside his
school? Was it hiding? If so, where?

Every second of every day, Calvin spent his time wondering
why?, thinking what?, and pondering how?

One day, Calvin heard the sound of loud banging coming from the garden shed. With great curiosity, he knocked on the shed door.

"Who's in there?" he shouted. "And what are you doing?"

The banging stopped for a second.

"It's only me," his Grandpa shouted back. "And I'm not telling you."

Then he carried on with his hammering and banging.

This just made Calvin more curious still. He decided to go and find his Dad. Perhaps he would know what Grandpa was doing.

Calvin's Dad was in the kitchen. And he was wearing a pinny!

"What are you doing in a pinny?" Calvin asked.

"Never you mind," replied his Dad, shooing him off into the living room. "Why don't you read a book or watch TV?"

Then his Dad rushed back into the kitchen and closed the door behind him.

Calvin listened curiously. He could hear the sounds of mixing and stirring. The oven timer was bleeping and his Dad seemed to be tutting loudly. What on earth was going on? He simply had to know!

Calvin went to find his Mum. Perhaps she could tell him. But he couldn't find her anywhere, and her car wasn't in the garage. Perhaps she'd gone to the shops? Or had taken the car to the carwash? Or had gone to visit his Aunty?

But she hadn't said anything about going anywhere. It was all very curious indeed.

Just then, a small van pulled into the drive. And out climbed a strange-looking man wearing a dark suit, a top hat and a long, shiny cape.

"Are you Calvin, young man?" he asked.

Calvin nodded. "And who are...?" he began.

Calvin's Dad came to the front door. "Ah good!" he said. "Right on time. Calvin, please will you help Mr Mysto unload his van. You can carry some of the boxes."

Calvin did as he was told. But, by now, he was positively bursting with curiosity.

"Who are you?" he said. "What are you doing here? What's in these boxes? And why are you wearing a hat and a cape?" he burbled. "Are you a magician?"

Mr Mysto smiled mysteriously but said nothing! Then Calvin's Mum pulled up in her car.

"Good!" thought Calvin. "Now Mum can tell me what's going on!"

But to Calvin's surprise, the car was full of his best friends.

"Mum!" he cried. "What are they doing here?"

His friends climbed out of the car.

"Everyone in the house," shouted Calvin's Mum.

Calvin couldn't contain himself a moment longer.

"Mum, Mum!" he demanded. "What's going on? Please tell me! Oh please! Please!"

"All in good time," his Mum replied.

She led him into the house, and into the front room. Mr Mysto and all Calvin's friends were already there.

Calvin's Grandpa was proudly holding a beautiful toy castle which he'd made himself in the garden shed.

And his Dad was standing by the table, which was laden down with food - sausages on sticks, egg and cress sandwiches, jelly and trifle. In the centre of the table stood a huge birthday cake!

So that's why he'd been wearing a pinny!

"Surprise!" they all cried. "Happy Birthday, Calvin!"

Calvin was very surprised. He'd been so busy wondering why, what and how, he'd completely forgotten that today was his birthday.

Look out for the next six Little Monsters!

HELPFUL HENRY

SHY SOPHIE

BOSSY BETHANY

REVOLTING RONNIE

WORRIED WINNIE

TV TREVOR

Cover printed Hexachrome, inner section printed 4 colour process by Speedprint (Leeds) Ltd. Tel: 0113 245 3665.